MYSTERY ON MUSHROOM ISLAND

MYSTERY ON MUSHROOM ISLAND

AN UNOFFICIAL MINECRAFTER MYSTERIES SERIES

BOOK SIX

Winter Morgan

Sky Pony Press
New York

This book is not authorized or sponsored by Microsoft Corp., Mojang AB, Notch Development AB or Scholastic Inc., or any other person or entity owning or controlling rights in the Minecraft name, trademark, or copyrights.

This book is not authorized or sponsored by Microsoft Corp., Mojang AB, Notch Development AB or Scholastic Inc., or any other person or entity owning or controlling rights in the Minecraft name, trademark, or copyrights.

Sky Pony Press books may be purchased in bulk at special discounts for sales promotion, corporate gifts, fund-raising, or educational purposes. Special editions can also be created to specifications. For details, contact the Special Sales Department, Sky Pony Press, 307 West 36th Street, 11th Floor, New York, NY 10018 or info@skyhorsepublishing.com.

Minecraft® is a registered trademark of Notch Development AB.
The Minecraft game is copyright © Mojang AB.

Visit our website at www.skyponypress.com.

10 9 8 7 6 5 4 3 2 1

Library of Congress Cataloging-in-Publication Data

Names: Morgan, Winter, author.
Title: Mystery on Mushroom Island / Winter Morgan.
Description: New York : Skyhorse Publishing, [2018]
Identifiers: LCCN 2018006608 (print) | LCCN 2018016292 (ebook) | ISBN 9781510731981 (eb) | ISBN 9781510731929 (pb)
Classification: LCC PZ7.1.M6698 (ebook) | LCC PZ7.1.M6698 My 2018 (print) | DDC [Fic]--dc23
LC record available at https://lccn.loc.gov/2018006608

Cover design by Brian Peterson
Cover photo by Megan Miller

Print ISBN: 978-1-5107-3192-9
Ebook ISBN: 978-1-5107-3198-1

Printed in Canada

TABLE OF CONTENTS

MYSTERY ON MUSHROOM ISLAND

1
ALL ABOARD

"She's here," Billy called out when he spotted Amira strolling down the sandy path outside Edison's house.

Billy had been waiting for Amira to return to Farmer's Bay all day and couldn't stop staring out the window to look for her. Amira hadn't been in Farmer's Bay in a while. She was living aboard a boat traveling around the Overworld. She had returned to Farmer's Bay only to pick up her friends for her big birthday celebration on Mushroom Island.

"She is? That's great!" Edison was in the middle of adding ingredients to potions at his brewing stand when Amira walked in the door. He rushed from the stand and raced to see his friend.

Amira asked, "Are you guys ready to go? The boat is docked, and I want to set sail before it gets dark. Erin and Peyton are already on the ship."

"Almost," Edison said as he pointed to a chest on the ground. "I just have to replenish my inventory. I also have to pack your present. That means you're going to have to leave so I can do that."

Amira giggled. "I guess I can do that," she said and walked outside with Billy. As they stood in front of the house, Puddles meowed at them, and Amira reached into her inventory for some fish.

"I think this ocelot knows I live at sea," Amira joked. "Puddles always seems to seek me out and beg for food."

Edison walked out of the house. "I'm ready for the birthday trip," he said with a smile.

"Great," Amira exclaimed. "Let's go. We also have to meet Omar and Anna on the ship. They are also joining us."

Edison was excited to go on a vacation with his friends. He felt as if the only time they left Farmer's Bay was when they had to solve a case or for a competition, and he was thrilled to have some time to just relax. He hadn't spent a lot of time on Mushroom Island, and he was eager to explore the scenic landscape and to gorge himself on mooshroom stew. He had only eaten it a few times, and each time he savored each bite. Mooshroom stew was hard to find in Farmer's Bay. You could only get it if someone you knew had visited Mushroom Island.

As they approached the shore, Edison noticed Anna's new ship. It was a small wooden ship with a sail. For a while she had been traveling on a massive boat, but this one was much smaller. "When did you get the new boat?"

"I built it when I was staying on Mushroom Island. Do you like it?" she asked.

"Yes, you did a great job," Edison said as he climbed aboard and looked around the immaculate ship. It was the ideal size to travel to Mushroom Island with his friends.

Amira wanted to set sail, but Anna and Omar had yet to arrive. She pointed at the setting sun. "This isn't good." She explained, "If they don't show up soon, we'll have to stay here for the night."

"You can stay at my house," Edison suggested. "I have more than enough room."

"Thanks," Amira replied, "but I really wanted to set sail tonight. There are people on Mushroom Island that are getting everything ready for the big party, and I wanted to be there to help them."

Edison had another idea. "Should we TP to Anna's house? Maybe they're still in Verdant Valley."

"That sounds good," said Amira. "What do you think, Billy?"

They agreed that TPing to Verdant Valley seemed like the wisest decision, and they TPed to Anna's house. When they arrived, she was pacing the length of her small home. She was shocked to see her friends spawn in front of her. "What are you doing here?" Anna asked them.

"Did you forget about the party? I have the boat docked in Farmer's Bay. We're supposed to celebrate my birthday," Amira reminded Anna.

Anna's voice shook as she spoke, and her eyes filled with tears. "I didn't, but something awful has happened."

"What's wrong?" asked Edison.

"I can't find Omar. It's been over two days," she explained. "Omar had been staying at the castle for the past month while he worked on adding an addition. I usually meet him at the end of the day, and we have dinner together. Two days ago, I went to see him, and he wasn't there. I figured he had something else to do and had forgotten to tell me, but it's been two days, and I haven't seen him anywhere. I'm really worried about him."

Edison replied that he would help, but before they had a chance to concoct a plan to find Omar, there was a banging on Anna's door.

"Omar?" Anna rushed to the door, but as she reached for the handle, the door ripped from its hinges, and a horrid odor filled the room.

"Zombies! Stand back!" Peyton hollered.

Edison and the others quickly suited up in their diamond armor, grabbed their swords, and leaped toward the three beasts that stood in Anna's doorway.

Anna pulled her sword from her inventory and struck a zombie that grabbed her arm. She fumbled with her sword and watched her weapon drop to the ground. Anna tried to pick it up, but she felt an incredible pain in her leg. An arrow had been shot through the open doorway and had struck her calf.

She tried to ignore the pain and pick up the dropped

sword, but the zombie lunged at her again, and she lost her last heart. Anna respawned in her bed in the midst of a zombie and skeleton battle in her living room. She pulled milk from her inventory to regain her strength while she lunged toward her sword, but it was missing. She had forgotten that when you drop something and are destroyed, you lose your item.

Anna plucked a wooden sword from her inventory and joined her friends in battle. She wanted the battle to end soon so they could have a meeting to find out what had happened to Omar. Sweat formed on her brow as she slammed her sword against a zombie.

Edison pulled potions from his inventory and splashed them on the undead, vacant-eyed creatures of the night filling the room while Billy, Amira, Peyton, and Erin sped toward the crop of skeletons that approached Anna's house. Anna fought alongside Edison using her wooden sword to weaken the zombies that Edison had doused with poison.

Edison splashed a zombie, and Anna delivered the final blow. Then they heard a familiar voice call out, "Help!"

2

STRANGE NIGHT

The residents of Verdant Valley heard Omar's cries through the sounds of battle. They crowded in the darkness on the grassy terrain as they defended themselves against the legions of zombies, skeletons, and creepers that now filled their town.

Anna could hear Omar's cries, but she couldn't see him. "Omar, where are you?" she called out to her friend.

"Help!" Omar hollered.

"We have to find him," Edison told Anna, but three zombies circled them, and they had to battle the smelly, undead mobs before they could search for their missing friend.

Anna slammed her wooden sword into the zombie. She knew she had to work twice as hard because she didn't have her diamond sword. The wooden sword lacked power, but she took a deep breath and used all of her force to plow the sword into the zombie's oozing stomach. One zombie was annihilated, but they had two more to destroy. Anna worried more would spawn and she wouldn't be able to find Omar in time. He needed help.

Edison swung his diamond sword into the second zombie and grabbed a bottle of potion to splash on the next beast. Anna was surprised when she destroyed the final zombie. The battle was easier than she imagined, and she bolted toward the sound of Omar's voice. However, the deeper they traveled into the dark night, the farther they seemed to be from Omar's voice. His voice grew fainter.

"We must have gone in the wrong direction," remarked Edison.

"How can that be?" questioned Anna. She was perplexed. They had run toward the sound of his voice.

"He must be running from someone," said Edison.

"But who?" asked Anna.

"We'll find out," Edison replied as five skeletons sprinted toward them and a barrage of arrows overwhelmed the duo. The skeletons instantly obliterated both of them. Anna respawned in her bed, but Edison was back in Farmer's Bay.

He looked up to see Puddles meowing, and he was shocked to see Omar in his living room. Omar stood by Edison's brewing stand and was taking potions and placing them in his inventory.

"What are you doing here?" questioned Edison. "Anna and I were trying to help you."

Omar was surprised. "Do you mind that I am taking some potions? I was going to leave a note and some emeralds."

"Don't worry about it," said Edison. "We're friends; you don't have to pay me. I just want to know who was attacking you. Anna and I heard you crying for help."

"Where?" Omar was shocked. "That wasn't me. I wasn't crying for help."

"In Verdant Valley," answered Edison.

"I wasn't in Verdant Valley. I had a quick job to construct an igloo in the cold biome, and I left town. I knew I had to be back for Amira's trip, and when I came back here, I found myself in the middle of a serious night invasion of hostile mobs. I had limited resources, so I came here to look for you. When you weren't here, I started to look for potions I could use to battle the hostile mobs."

Zombies ripped the hinges off Edison's door, and Puddles meowed. Edison sprinted toward the zombies armed with potion in one hand and his sword in the other. He splashed the first zombie that lumbered into the small living room and then pierced it with his diamond sword. Omar doused the zombie with potion until it was weakened and destroyed. Edison picked up the rotten flesh the zombie dropped to the ground.

Omar used the remainder of his potions to splash the two zombies walking into the dark living room. As he sprayed the zombies, the sun rose, and the zombies faded.

"That was a crazy night," Edison said as he let out a breath. He was exhausted. He added, "Anna will be happy to see you. She was worried about you. She said you were missing."

"Missing?" Omar looked confused. "Why did she think that?"

"She had been looking for you in town and didn't know where you were. She said you'd been hanging out after you finished your work on the castle and one day she went to look for you and you were gone."

"I went to her house to tell her I was leaving for the cold biome, but she wasn't there, so I left a note. The note said she should meet me on Amira's boat. She must have not seen it," explained Omar.

"Let's TP to Anna's house. They are all there. We should get ready and head to the boat. I know that Amira has a lot of different activities planned for the party on Mushroom Island."

"Yes," Omar said, "I want her to see I'm okay. I feel bad that she was worried about me."

"Before we go, we should fill up our inventories with some potions," said Edison as he grabbed a bunch of potions from the case where he had stored the potions for his brewing stand. He wasn't going to work at the brewing stand this week because he was going on vacation. Since he wasn't planning on working at the stand, he hadn't brewed that much, and the case was almost empty. "I didn't realize I was so low on potions. Maybe I should brew a few before we leave?"

"Do we have time?" asked Omar. "We should really

TP to Annie's house. I don't want her to worry about me."

"Annie?" questioned Edison.

"I'm sorry, I meant . . ." Omar paused, and he never had a chance to correct himself because his name was being called.

"Omar!" Anna exclaimed. "You're here!"

"Did you save him?" asked Peyton.

Billy, Erin, Peyton, Amira, and Anna stood in the living room. They were excited to be reunited, and they all spoke at once. This irritated Omar, and he screamed, "Be quiet, everyone! You're so loud."

"Are you okay?" asked Anna.

Edison thought this was unusual behavior. Omar was always very laid back and never shouted at anyone.

Omar apologized. "I'm sorry, I'm very tired. I haven't slept for two days. I was very busy trying to finish an igloo that I was asked to construct. I was trying to finish it before we had to leave for Mushroom Island."

"Don't worry," Amira said. "Soon we'll be on Mushroom Island, and we can all relax."

The gang walked to the boat. Edison couldn't stop thinking about Omar's unusual behavior. He had never shouted before, and he had worked tirelessly on other projects. They had been involved in very intense situations, and Omar had always been the calm one. He also had forgotten Anna's name. He called her Annie. Edison thought this was very strange since they were very close. They had been living as neighbors in Verdant Valley the whole time Omar worked on the castle, and Edison couldn't imagine Omar forgetting a friend's name.

Edison decided to keep a close eye on Omar. As they walked down the sandy path toward the shore, he walked alongside Omar, trying to see if there was anything strange about his behavior.

"We have to hurry," Amira informed them as they reached the shore. "The trip is a lot longer than you think, and I want to get there in time for the mooshroom stew festival."

"The mooshroom stew festival?" Billy questioned. "That sounds like fun. What's that?"

"It's an annual festival where people from all around the Overworld celebrate the tasty mooshroom stew. I specifically timed my party to occur during this festival. It's so much fun."

They hopped aboard the boat, and as they set sail toward Mushroom Island, Edison stared at Omar chatting with Anna. He wondered if Anna noticed anything strange about her good friend. He made a note to ask Anna.

Erin and Amira walked over to Anna and Omar and started talking about mooshroom stew. Amira asked, "Have you guys ever had it?"

Anna told them about a large portion of mooshroom stew she had once stored in her inventory. She remembered how sad she was when she finished it off. "It's one of my favorites," she declared.

"Mine too," said Amira. "This festival is going to be so much fun. I hope this boat can travel a bit faster.

It's hard to guess when we'll get there because so much depends on the wind. Remember when we were sailing across the Overworld returning all of that stolen treasure and we got stuck in the middle of the ocean because the boat broke down?" she said to Omar. They had once traveled around the Overworld together for many months.

Omar smiled but didn't say anything. This bothered Amira. "Do you not remember?"

"I do," he said. "Of course I do."

Edison was listening to their conversation as he looked out at the deep blue ocean that seemed endless. He tried to relax, but he couldn't stop thinking about Omar.

Billy walked over to him. "Are you excited for this vacation?"

Edison smiled and replied, "Yes." He reminded himself that this was a vacation and he should stop playing detective. He had to stop questioning if something seemed suspicious with his old friend Omar. Instead, he should enjoy the view, soak in the sun, and feel the ocean breeze in his hair. He was starting to relax when he heard Anna correct Omar. "Her name is Erin, not Arlene."

When Edison heard these words, he knew he was about to embark on another case.

3
SEABOUND

The wind stopped, and the boat slowed down. "You have to help me, Omar," said Amira. "You're the only one onboard who has experience navigating a boat."

Omar stood by Amira as she tried to move the boat forward to Mushroom Island. "Aren't you going to help me?" she asked.

"Yes." Omar appeared confused. "It's just been a long time since I've helped you at sea. I've been so busy building in Verdant Land."

"Verdant Land?" questioned Anna. "You mean Verdant Valley?"

"Yes." Omar touched his forehead. "I don't feel that well. Is there a space where I can rest? I think I was injured during the battle. My memory seems to be going on me. Maybe I was poisoned? I had some of your potions to regain my strength, Edison, do you think that one of your potions might have caused this? Maybe you made a mistake."

Edison's mouth gaped open. He couldn't believe Omar was placing the blame on him. "No, I've used all of the potions I've brewed. I test each one."

"You test every potion?" Omar laughed. "That seems impossible."

"I know that I've ingested something from all of the batches of potions that you borrowed," Edison said, defending himself. "Something is different with you, Omar. You keep messing up people's names, and you don't remember how to drive a boat. I find it all suspicious."

Omar coughed. "I'm sorry. I didn't mean to blame you. I think I must be sick. I must have come down with something when I was in the cold biome." He leaned his head against the ship's railing.

"Be careful," Anna advised him. "It's not good to be so close to the edge. You don't want to fall overboard."

"I'll be fine," Omar said. "I just need a few minutes to rest."

Billy walked over to Edison and whispered, "Everything isn't a potential case. Our friend is sick, and you questioned him about his errors. You have to just relax and enjoy the vacation."

Edison signaled to Billy that they should move to a quieter part of the ship. "I'm telling you, I have a feeling in my gut that something isn't right with Omar. It just seems very odd that he forgot people's names, and he called Verdant Valley 'Verdant Land.' I am going to watch him."

"That's fine, but I don't want it ruining your vacation. I want you to enjoy being on Mushroom Island. Remember, this is Amira's big birthday celebration. We've all worked very hard the last year solving all sorts of cases, and I think we all need a vacation," said Billy.

Anna approached them. "What are you guys whispering about?"

"It's nothing," Billy replied.

"No, it isn't nothing," said Edison. "We have to tell her."

"Tell me what?" asked Anna.

"It's nothing," said Billy.

"It's something." Edison was angry. "I think there's something going on with Omar. Remember last night when we heard his voice? When I respawned in my bungalow, Omar was in my bungalow going through my potions. I found it very strange, because we had just heard him in Verdant Valley," said Edison.

"That is strange," said Anna.

"Let's not make something out of nothing," said Billy. "I'm here to enjoy a vacation. I don't want to play detective. I feel like we've done that enough."

"Okay," Anna said. "Why don't we just watch Omar? If he acts strangely, then we'll start investigating. For now, we'll just say he's sick."

Edison agreed. "Okay, but if there is anything that is out of the ordinary, I will start questioning him."

Billy walked over to Omar. "Are you feeling better?"

Omar stared at the ocean as he spoke. "Yes, I do feel a lot better." He pulled an apple from his inventory and took a bite. "I was feeling sick before, but I think I'll be fine. I must be working too hard. All of this building is tiring me out."

"I get it," said Billy. "I feel the same way about being a detective. We worked on so many cases, and I just want to focus on my treasure hunting."

"Yes," Omar said. "Ollie, you shouldn't try to be a detective like your friend over there, the alchemist. Just relax. You're on vacation."

Billy didn't correct Omar. He didn't tell him that his name was Billy or let him know that Edison's name was Edison. He just took note of this odd interaction. He wasn't going to tell Edison and Anna. He didn't want to ruin this rare vacation.

Amira called out, "The boat is moving at a great pace. We're almost at Mushroom Island."

Edison stood next to Amira and looked out at the large, bright-colored mushrooms sprouting from the island. He was intoxicated by the stunning view of the scenic island. He decided that he wouldn't bother investigating Omar, but would just enjoy his time on vacation.

"Can you hear the sound of music?" asked Amira. "That's the festival. It's going to be so much fun."

The sounds of a drum beating vibrated against the boat. Edison's heart raced as they approached the shore. He hadn't realized how much he needed a vacation until they approached the lively, peaceful island.

"I hear there's a contest where people compete to see who can eat the most mooshroom stew," said Anna.

"Really? That's awesome," exclaimed Peyton. "I'm totally in."

"Me too!" added Erin.

"I guess we're going to be competitors." Peyton smiled.

"Bring it on!" Erin said.

"I wonder what you win," questioned Billy.

Amira called out to Omar, "Are you feeling better? Can you help me dock the boat?"

Omar replied, "I'll try. I am feeling a bit better."

Amira and Omar steered the boat toward the dock. There were many people walking around the dock area. Edison could see a group of people dancing by a pasture filled with mooshrooms. Edison watched as Omar carefully helped Amira put down the anchor and dock the boat at Mushroom Island.

Omar smiled at Amira. "We're going to have a lot of fun for your birthday."

"I hope so!" Amira exclaimed.

Edison watched this exchange and felt much better about Omar. Maybe he *was* just feeling sick, or perhaps somebody *had* injured him and it left his memory impaired. He had heard Omar call for help. Edison wished he was able to see who was hurting Omar when he was screaming for them in Verdant Valley, but it had been so dark, and they couldn't see anything.

Edison was distracted from his thoughts when he watched Peyton push Erin out of the way and try to be the first person off the boat.

"May the best person win," Peyton said as she

climbed down the ladder and sprinted toward the festival.

"Wait up!" Erin called out to her friend.

Edison had never seen Erin and Peyton act this way, and he wondered if everyone was just a bit off. He climbed down the ladder. As he reached the ground, he could smell the mooshroom stew.

"Do you smell that?" he asked Billy.

"Yes," said Billy. "It smells lovely. Should we get a bowl, or should we sign up for the competitive eating competition?"

"I think I'll pass on the contest. I just want to relax. But we should go and cheer on Peyton and Erin."

Billy agreed, and they walked to the center of the festival with Amira and Omar. Amira told them about where they were staying.

"My friend has a large house, and she invited us to stay with her," said Amira.

"Who's your friend?" asked Billy.

"Her name is Allyson," said Amira.

"Allyson. Does she have red hair?" asked Omar.

"Yes, do you know her?" asked Amira.

Omar paused and then fumbled with his words when he said, "Um, I don't. I thought I heard you mention her."

As they entered the festival, Edison looked back for Omar, but he was gone.

4
MOOSHROOM STEW FESTIVAL

"Where's Omar?" questioned Edison.

Amira looked around. "That's strange. He was just next to me. He must have rushed ahead into the festival."

Edison wanted to find Omar, but a woman with pink hair held a megaphone and walked through the crowd announcing the mooshroom stew eating contest was about to begin.

"Who will be declared the winner?" she asked as she walked around the festival. "Cheer on your friends!"

Billy pointed to the stage. Peyton and Erin were standing next to each other. In front of them was a long table filled with what seemed like a never-ending supply of bowls filled with mooshroom stew. The woman with the pink hair kept shouting into the megaphone, trying to gather a crowd to watch the contest. When she felt there were enough people paying attention to the upcoming competition, she stepped onto the stage.

"These brave folks have decided to participate in the mooshroom stew competition. Are there any other people in the audience who would like to join them? There are only nine people up here, and we have room for ten."

Billy looked at Amira. "You should do it. You love mooshroom stew."

"I don't like being on stage. I'm very shy," she confessed. "Can you do it?"

"You think I should?" Billy asked his friends.

"Why not?" questioned Edison. "I bet it's a lot of fun."

The woman with the megaphone said, "Doesn't anybody want to do it? We can't begin the competition until we have one more person."

Billy raised his hand. "I'll do it!"

"Great!" exclaimed the woman with the megaphone.

Billy raced to the stage and walked to the empty space as the woman with the megaphone began to announce the rules.

"When I say 'begin,' you start drinking the bowls of mooshroom stew, and when I say 'stop,' you guys stop. The judges will walk by and count the bowls. The person who has the largest number of empty bowls is the winner. Okay, you guys ready?" She looked at the contestants.

Edison was excited to see his three friends on stage, but he was distracted because he still couldn't see Omar in the crowd. The Omar he knew would be at the front of the stage cheering them on, but there was something off about Omar. Edison felt like the person they had traveled to Mushroom Island with was not Omar, but an imposter. He didn't want to confront Omar, but he had to find out if this was true.

"Ready, set, go!" exclaimed the woman with the megaphone, and the group of ten contestants drank the stew.

Edison couldn't imagine gorging himself with mooshroom stew. Yet watching his friend's compete made him quite hungry. He craved a bowl of mooshroom stew as he cheered his friends. "Go, guys!"

He watched Billy devour bowls of stew and couldn't keep track of how many each one of them had eaten. The woman with the megaphone called out, "Stop." The judges walked the length of the stage, stopping in front of each participant and counting the empty bowls.

"We have a winner!" exclaimed the woman with pink hair.

A judge walked over to Peyton. "Congratulations! You're our first place winner."

Peyton smiled. "That's amazing. I'm so happy."

The judge presented Peyton with a golden apple. "This is your prize. I know these come in handy during zombie invasions, but you won't need it here. There are no hostile mobs on Mushroom Island. So just enjoy yourself and know that you have this in your inventory for your return home. You did a great job!"

Erin, Peyton, and Billy walked off the stage. Edison congratulated them, "You guys are all winners to me."

"You're so cheesy." Billy laughed. "That sounds like something a parent would say to a kid."

"Well, I was impressed watching you in the competition," Edison said. "And now I'm in the mood for a bowl of mooshroom stew."

Peyton put her hand in front of her mouth. "Please, just thinking about ever eating that again makes me sick. It's funny, I used to love it, but now I feel like I can never eat it again."

"I know how you feel," said Billy.

"Me too," added Erin.

Anna asked, "So was it worth it?"

"Yeah, it was fun," said Erin.

Amira said, "I was too afraid to go on stage. It was fun watching you guys."

Edison's mind was still focused on food. "Are you guys really that disgusted by the mooshroom stew? If so, I might have to dine alone. I really want a bowl," he said.

"I do too," Amira said.

"So do I," added Anna.

Amira suggested, "Why don't we get one while you guys explore the rest of the festival? Do you see that big rollercoaster? It looks like so much fun."

"I can't go on a rollercoaster right now." Erin rubbed her stomach. "It's hard to walk. I just need to rest."

"That competition was very intense, wasn't it?" asked Amira.

The competitors nodded their heads in unison.

Amira pulled out a map from her inventory. "This is the map to Allyson's house. You guys should go there and rest. My friend Allyson is putting together a feast for tonight, so she should be there now. She has a lot to prepare. We'll meet you later."

Edison, Anna, and Amira walked through the fair. They ate bowls of mooshroom stew and looked at the all of the rides.

"We should go on the Ferris wheel," suggested Anna.

"We have to find Omar," said Edison.

"He wasn't feeling well," said Anna. "Maybe he went to the beach to rest? I know you're very suspicious of him, and I do think it's odd that he called me by the wrong name."

They were shocked when Omar walked over to them. "Omar," Anna said, "we were worried about you."

"I was just walking around, Annie. Don't worry," Omar replied.

Anna didn't correct him, but she caught his error. This was another time he messed up her name. Omar's behavior was incredibly suspicious.

"You seem like you're still not feeling well," said Amira. "Why don't you go to my friend Allyson's house to rest?" She pulled out another map from her inventory and showed Omar the way to get there.

Omar thanked her and held the map as he walked in the direction of Allyson's house.

When he was out of earshot, Anna said, "I agree he's still acting off. Let's see if he feels better after resting at Allyson's house. Right now, I just want to enjoy this festival. We never get to go on rides and eat a bunch of food. I want to have fun."

"So do I," Amira said as she raced toward the line for the Ferris wheel.

As they each climbed into their own cars on the massive Ferris wheel, Edison looked out and thought he saw Omar, which he found strange, because Omar was supposed to be heading to Allyson's house. He told himself that he was probably wrong because it was hard to make out the people on the ground. They seemed so small, almost like little toy people. He tried to simply enjoy the view as he reached the top. Mushroom Island was a beautiful place. He could see the shoreline and the boat docked on the peaceful water.

Red mushrooms dotted the green landscape, and Edison took a deep breath and relaxed as he went around on the Ferris wheel. There was a slight breeze, and the sun shone brightly in the sky. Everything seemed peaceful until the Ferris wheel shook violently as a loud boom thundered through the sky.

People were screaming as smoke filled the air.

"What was that?" Anna screamed.

"I think there was an explosion," said Amira.

Edison wanted to get off the ride, but he had to wait for all of the other cars to be emptied. It felt like an eternity as he waited to exit the Ferris wheel. He could see Anna and Amira waiting for him. The smoke was fading a bit, but people were still running away from the festival.

"What do you think happened?" asked Amira.

"I don't know, but we're going to find out," said Edison.

As he spoke, another explosion shook the ground.

"Again! What is going on?" Edison screamed.

He couldn't hear a reply because a third explosion rocked the festival.

5
QUESTIONS AND CURSES

When the smoke faded and there wasn't another explosion, people calmed down, and Edison could actually make out passing conversations.

"I think this island is cursed," an older woman dressed in a shawl told her friend.

Her friend, who had dark gray hair and wore a black dress, eagerly remarked, "Yes, I've heard about that curse. They said there would be three explosions, and then we'd have lots of trouble."

Edison excused himself. "I'm sorry. I don't want to interrupt, but what is the story behind the curse?"

The woman in the shawl was more than happy to tell Edison, Anna, and Amira about the curse. "I've lived on Mushroom Island my entire life. I've never left and never seen a hostile mob. Most of my family hasn't. When I was younger, I'd tell my parents that I wanted to see the rest of the Overworld, but they would tell me how scary it was and describe zombies with oozing flesh and skeletons that shot arrows at you, and it scared me a lot.

"I was happy to live on Mushroom Island forever until my brother told me that one day our island would see all of the horrors of the Overworld. There was a curse an old traveler put on our island when he had a fight with a farmer who lived here. Once my brother told me this, I was always worried about the curse. However, a lot of people said it was just a story and it would never happen. I never thought it would until this happened.

"My brother said that the curse would start with three explosions, and that's just what happened. There were three explosions." She let out a small cough and wrapped the shawl around her frail body.

"What else will happen?" asked Edison.

"I just told you, we would be attacked by hostile mobs. All of the horrible monsters that live in all of the biomes will spawn here and attack us."

Edison, Amira, and Anna didn't believe in curses, but they weren't going to tell the older woman this fact. Instead, Edison thanked her for telling them the story about the curse and added, "I hope these mobs don't spawn."

"They will," the woman said. "Unfortunately, they will." And the two older women walked off into the crowd.

Amira suggested they go to Allyson's house. "We

should see how our friends are, and also it looks like one of the explosions took place near the house."

The trio sprinted toward Allyson's house, which had a sandy surface and a red roof. Its design was inspired by the landscape, and it didn't look as if it was constructed, but rather appeared as if it sprouted from the ground.

Amira spotted Allyson standing in front of the house. Allyson called out, "Are you guys okay?"

"Yes," Amira replied. When they approached the house, Amira introduced her friends to Allyson and then asked, "Did my other friends show up?"

"Yes, Peyton, Erin, and Billy are here," Allyson replied.

"What about Omar?" asked Edison.

"I never met anybody by that name," Allyson said. "Was he supposed to be here?"

Amira's voice shook. She was worried about Omar. "I hope he's okay. I hope he didn't get hurt in any of the explosions."

"Or cause them," muttered Edison.

"Edison!" Amira screamed. "How can you say that? I know you think he's been acting strangely, but you can't say that he's responsible for these horrific explosions."

"I think we should go look for him," said Anna. "I don't know if he's behind these attacks, but I do know he's missing and he's my good friend, and I must find him."

Allyson pointed to a cave in the distance. Smoke billowed from the cave. "That's where there was one explosion. I don't think anybody was hurt. Nobody ever goes into that cave. There aren't any minerals left in the cave because we mined from it for such a long time. It hasn't been occupied in years."

"I wonder how it exploded," said Anna.

"It's the curse," Edison joked.

Amira and Anna laughed, but Allyson interrupted their laughter. "Please don't make fun of the curse. It's a part of our island's folklore. I think it's more than a coincidence that there were three explosions."

"There was an older woman who told us that after the three explosions, all of the hostile mobs from the Overworld would attack the people on Mushroom Island," said Anna.

"Yes." Allyson bit her lip. "I'm very concerned that we are about to be attacked."

"I don't believe in these sorts of stories," said Edison. "I'm sorry to admit that, but I don't think anyone or anyplace can be cursed."

"I know it sounds unlikely, but we have to be prepared," Allyson said.

Edison tried to contain his laughter, but he couldn't believe a good friend of Amira's could actually believe in curses.

He didn't feel like laughing when he heard a loud roar and looked up in the sky to see an Ender Dragon flying swiftly in circles, as if searching for prey.

6
DRAGON'S BREATH

"And you guys thought I was crazy for believing in curses," Allyson screamed as she pulled armor and a diamond sword from her inventory and raced toward the muscular flying menace.

She fearlessly ripped into the belly of the beast and then raced back to her house to shelter herself from the purple fire–breathing dragon. She told them, "You guys have to help us battle these hostile mobs and mob bosses. Many of the natives have never fought in their lives. They haven't even seen a mob."

Edison, Amira, and Anna were suited up and had their swords. Anna looked down at her wooden sword. She knew it wasn't powerful enough to damage the Ender Dragon. Edison pulled a diamond sword from his inventory. "Take this. I have an extra onc."

Anna was usually the one who handed out supplies. She always had a chest filled with armor and swords that she lent people when they had lost their weapons and other resources. It felt strange to take something from her friend when she was the one who was always the one helping others.

The trio called for their friends, and Billy, Peyton, and Erin sprinted from the house and joined them in a battle against one of the most powerful creatures in the universe.

"One of us should stay by the house and shoot arrows at the dragon. If we pound the beast with arrows, we'll be able to weaken it," Anna ordered the others.

Amira told Allyson, "It's easier to battle an Ender Dragon here than in the End because there aren't any crystals that the dragon can eat to regain its strength."

"Well, I don't think this is easy," Allyson declared as she slammed her sword into the dragon's wing and then lurched away from the fireball the dragon spit from its mouth. The dragon was focused on destroying Allyson, and it picked up its pace as it charged toward her. She was helpless. Her health bar was already low from battling the dragon, and one hit would destroy her. Allyson pushed her yellow hair from her eyes. Sweat dripped down her face as she sprinted to her house. Allyson felt an unnatural pain radiate down her back, and she cried out in agony, "Ouch!"

Despite wearing the armor, the final attack from the dragon was fatal, and Allyson respawned in her bed. She could hear friends in the midst of the battle. The dragon's wing ripped into the side of her house and made a gaping hole in her red roof. Allyson rushed outside and hurried to Edison, who pierced the side of the dragon and then splashed a potion that the weakened monster.

"Just keep shooting arrows," Edison called out to his friends.

Billy, Erin, and Peyton tirelessly shot arrows and the beast, leaving the dragon incredibly vulnerable to a strike from a sword. Amira, Anna, and Edison ripped into the dragon's belly with their swords. This final blow destroyed the beast. As it vanished, it left a dragon egg behind and a portal to the End.

Edison stared at the portal. Billy sprinted toward him and breathlessly remarked, "This isn't the time to go the End."

"We have to be prepared for what comes next," said Allyson. "Maybe we can set up a place where we can hold a meeting and offer tips to natives of Mushroom Island that have never met a hostile mob. We can teach them how to battle the mobs."

"I can teach them how to brew potions that will help them defeat the mobs," exclaimed Edison. He liked the idea of teaching people how to brew. He missed alchemy even though it had been only a couple days since he brewed potions. He still felt an absence when he wasn't in front of the brewing station.

Amira said, "I don't think we have time for that. I don't even think we should hold a meeting. I think we should just try to figure out how to stop the curse."

Anna asked, "Allyson, do you know if there is an

end to the story of the curse? Did they ever say what had to be done to have things go back to normal?"

Allyson paused. "I don't know. I only know the story about the three explosions and the hostile mobs. Perhaps we could try to find the farmer who the traveler cursed."

"Yes," said Billy, "we need more information to help us stop this curse."

Allyson said, "I know a bunch of farmers, but they're on the other side of the island. Maybe we should start there?"

"Yes," said Anna, "that sounds like a good idea."

Allyson led them toward the farms and walked by the cave, which still had a steady stream of smoke coming out of it.

"Do you think we should look inside?" questioned Billy.

Edison walked toward the entrance. "It's still rather smoky. I don't think it's a great idea."

"We need to see if there are any clues," said Anna. "I know it seems dangerous, but we should go inside."

Edison didn't want to explore a smoky cave and the aftermath of an explosion, but he did know they needed to search for clues. Even though the Ender Dragon had spawned, he still didn't believe in curses.

As they entered the cave, he took a deep breath and told himself that it would be okay. He almost convinced himself that everything would be fine until they heard a voice shout at them through the smoky darkness.

"Who's there?" the nameless voice demanded.

7
CREEPERS IN THE CAVE

"We're here to help," Allyson told the voice. "We just want to see what happened and if anybody was in here."

"Go away!" the person called out. The voice was high-pitched, and it sounded as if they had difficulty breathing. They took a deep breath between every word they spoke.

"You sound like you're not able to breathe," said Amira. "Do you need help getting out of the cave?"

A small woman who wore a striped dress and had violet hair walked toward them. "I can breathe fine, but I just want to be left alone."

Allyson recognized her from Mushroom Island. "I know you. You live down the road from me. You're Greta, right?"

"Yes," Greta replied.

"What are you doing in here?" asked Anna.

"None of your business," said Greta.

Edison and Billy didn't talk to the woman, but walked deeper into the cave. Through the thick smoke, Edison looked down at the ground and saw the explosion had cracked a large hole in the blocky dirt that was teeming with blue diamonds.

"This is why Greta doesn't want to leave," said Billy.

"Get away from there!" Greta shouted.

"This isn't your cave," Edison said. "Anybody can mine here."

"But I discovered it first," declared Greta. "It's all mine."

Allyson looked at the hole. "Wow, this is weird. I spent my entire life mining in this cave. We dug deeper than this and there weren't any minerals left. I wonder how so many more sprouted in the cave."

"I don't know, and I don't care," said Greta. "I just want all of these treasures. I deserve them."

Billy spotted a pair of red eyes staring at him from the dark musty cave. "A cave spider!" he warned the others. With his diamond sword, he rushed toward the cave-dwelling mob and destroyed the spider. The spider dropped an eye that Billy handed to Edison. "For your potions."

Greta stood by in awe. "How did you do that?"

"It was easy. I've destroyed a lot of spiders," said Billy. "I can show you how. It's not hard to learn."

"Really?" questioned Greta. "I've never seen a hostile mob in my life."

"Well, get ready to see a lot of them," said Allyson.

"Why?" Greta asked.

Allyson explained, "I believe these three explosions are linked to the curse on the island. We were just on our way to speak to the farmers about the curse when we passed by the cave and decided to see if anyone was in here or if there were any clues to help us figure out how to stop hostile mobs from forming on the island."

"I don't believe in that story. I've been hearing about it for years, and it just seems like utter nonsense," said Greta.

"It's not nonsense," Allyson declared. "It's happening."

Greta didn't listen and climbed into the hole, pulled out a pickaxe, and began to dig into the ground. "Diamonds, diamonds, diamonds," she called out as she gathered a handful of diamonds and placed them in her inventory.

"Watch out!" Anna screamed.

Greta had no idea what was lurking behind her. Two green creepers exploded before she had a chance to turn around or get advice from Billy on how to annihilate the explosive mob.

"Greta!" Allyson called out, but Greta had been destroyed.

"Oh no!" Peyton screamed as the small smoky cave filled with creepers.

"Did someone place a spawner here?" asked Edison. "There are just too many creepers." He pulled a potion out of his inventory and splashed the mobs as the group raced from the cave. A trail of green creepers silently followed them out of the smoky cave and into the lush, green, grassy path that led toward the farms.

"We have to escape from the creepers," said Erin.

"How far does that cave go back?" asked Billy.

Allyson said, "Not very far, and there's no stronghold. I wonder where they could have placed a monster spawner?"

"Maybe they aren't being spawned from a monster spawner, but they're a part of the curse," suggested Erin.

Edison was still leery of curses. He knew there had to be someone behind this attack on Mushroom Island, and he was going to find out who. But first they had to defeat the cluster of creepers that were trying to destroy them.

"Let's use our bow and arrows," suggested Amira.

The gang shot arrows and threw potions on the creepers, defeating the mobs without being destroyed. They felt victorious. As they jogged toward the farm to question the farmers, they heard a familiar voice call out, "Wait for me!"

8

NIGHT FIGHT

"Omar," Amira said, "where have you been? We were worried about you."

"I couldn't find your friend's house, and when I finally did find it, nobody was there," he explained. Then he asked, "Where are you going? I thought there was going to be a big birthday feast tonight."

"Mushroom Island is in trouble. We have to help everyone," explained Amira. "We have to find out what's happening with the curse."

"What curse? What are you talking about?" asked Omar.

"Just follow us. We don't have time to explain," Amira told him.

Allyson introduced herself to Omar, and then they sprinted toward the farm. When they reached the first farm, it was empty, and all of the mooshrooms were missing. The mushrooms sprouting from the ground had been picked, and the farmhouse was emptied.

"What happened here?" asked Allyson.

"I have no idea." Edison inspected the farm. "It looks like someone has ruined this farm. We should head to the next farm."

The sun was beginning to set, which wouldn't have been an issue on Mushroom Island before, but now that the hostile mobs were spawning, they were vulnerable to attacks.

"Does everyone have a fully stocked inventory?" asked Edison. "We have to be prepared for a long night battle. We have no idea what is going to come next. We already had to battle the Ender Dragon."

Allyson said, "I'm worried about all of the natives. Look at Greta. She was in awe of Billy destroying a spider. What will she do when she comes face to face with a spider jockey?"

"The best way we can help the folks of Mushroom Island is by stopping this attack. We should go to the next farm and question the farmer. We need more information," Edison said.

The group sprinted behind Allyson as they reached the neighboring farm, which was also in shambles. A lone farmer stood by the farmhouse. She called out to them, "Someone robbed my farm and took all of my mooshrooms."

"Did you see what they looked like?" asked Allyson.

"No, when I came back from the festival, I found that all of my mooshrooms were missing, and someone stole all of my diamonds from my chest in my house," she cried.

"We're here to help you," Amira reassured her. "We believe this is all a part of the curse. Do you happen to know anything about it? We were told that an old traveler once put a curse on a farmer."

"Yes," she replied, "that was me."

"What's your name?" asked Allyson.

"Dina," she replied, "One day a traveler came by and wanted to buy my mooshrooms, put them on a boat, and to bring them to spots all across the Overworld so everyone could have mooshroom stew. I am very protective of my mooshrooms, and I said he couldn't have them. I told him they were special to Mushroom Island and if he wanted the stew, he'd have to travel here."

"When did he put a curse on you, Dina?" asked Allyson.

"I told him that he couldn't have the mooshrooms, and he told me that my island would be cursed and one day there would be three explosions and then we'd have the same problems that all of the Overworld had, and we'd have hostile mobs. He said we'd never be able to go out at night because we'd be attacked by zombies and skeletons."

Before Dina could continue with the rest of the story. Four skeletons spawned and shot arrows at the gang. Dina wasn't wearing any armor, so the arrows pierced her chest. She cried out in pain as she lost a heart.

"Are those skeletons?" she asked.

"Yes," Allyson said. "Don't worry, we'll show you how to destroy them. Do you have any weapons?"

"No," Dina replied as she raced back inside her farmhouse to shelter herself from the attack.

Allyson and Amira followed Dina into the house. They wanted to help her battle the hostile mobs that would spawn throughout the night.

Edison, Billy, Anna, Peyton, and Erin sprinted toward the skeletons and swung their diamond swords at the bony beasts. As the friends ripped into the rattling bones, the skeletons lost all of their hearts and were destroyed. The gang picked up the dropped bones.

"Some vacation," Edison joked as he picked up the bones.

"We have to stop these attacks," said Billy. "I know we can do it."

As they walked back to Dina's house, they kept a close eye out for hostile mobs that might spawn near the farm. Peyton looked around and asked, "What happened to Omar?"

Edison replied, "Maybe he's with Amira and Allyson in Dina's house."

When they entered the house, they didn't see Omar. "Where's Omar?" asked Billy.

"I thought he was with you guys," said Amira.

"Oh no." Anna was worried. "I hope he's okay. He was acting so off."

Amira suggested they search for Omar, but Edison said, "We will find him, but first we should talk to Dina about the traveler."

Edison didn't want to get sidetracked. He knew that they had to find out more details from Dina. "Tell us everything about the traveler."

"I didn't know him that well. He just came here, and when I refused to give him the mooshrooms, he was very upset. He shouted at me. I didn't fight back, because there was nothing to say. When I didn't respond, he got very upset, and that's when he put a curse on me."

"What did he look like?" asked Edison.

"He had yellow hair and glasses. I'm sorry," she apologized, "but I don't remember what he was wearing. I do remember that he coughed a lot. I thought he was sick."

"Coughed a lot. Well, that's a start," said Billy.

"Do you think anyone else on Mushroom Island knows him?" asked Amira.

Dina paused and then replied, "I think some people in town knew him better. He spent a lot of time in the village trading stuff. We love when people come and trade resources because ours are so limited on the island."

"I don't think we should travel to town now. It's dark out, and we have to get your inventory filled with all of the supplies needed for battling hostile mobs," said Amira.

"Don't bother," said Dina. "I don't even know what to do with a weapon. I've never been in battle. I'm not going to be much of a help."

"We will help you," said Anna. "Just follow what we do and try and keep up, and I think you'll be okay."

"I don't know to fight." Dina's voice cracked, and she was so nervous she could barely get the words out.

"Don't worry, Dina. You'll feel much better when you put this on." Edison pulled armor from his inventory.

"Really?" Dina asked as she looked at the armor.

"Yes, I have an extra one."

Dina held the shiny diamond armor, inspecting it, "This is very nice. I don't know how to wear it."

Amira showed her how to place the armor on her body. "This is the first step to battle. You have to be prepared."

"Thank you." Dina looked down at the armor. "I feel a lot stronger now."

"Now you're going to get a crash course on how to battle mobs, but you're going to have to help us stop the traveler who put a curse on the island," said Allyson.

"I never left Mushroom Island because I never wanted to see a hostile mob, and now I'm probably going to see every one that exists in the Overworld," she said in one breath. As she spoke, a gang of zombies ripped her farmhouse door from its hinges. "Who are they? What's that smell?"

"This is your first zombie battle," said Amira. "Are you ready?"

9

WITHER OR NOT, HERE I COME

The smell of rotting flesh filled the room, and Dina cried out, "The smell! I can't take the smell."

"Don't let it distract you," Edison advised. "Just use the sword. You can do it."

Edison splashed a potion on the zombies, and Dina cowered behind him. Anna leaped toward a zombie, ripping into its belly with her diamond sword. Dina tried to fight. She mimicked Anna's move and was shocked when she destroyed the undead beast with one hit.

"Great job, Dina!" Anna pointed to the rotten flesh on the ground. "Pick that up, you've earned it."

Dina was confident after easily destroying the zombie. However, that feeling quickly faded when she looked up and saw an army of zombies lumbering through her door. She watched as Amira, Anna, and the others fearlessly fought the smelly creatures.

Dina took a deep breath and reminded herself that she should just follow the others and she'd be okay.

A zombie grabbed Dina's arm, and she lost a heart. She fumbled with her sword but regained control of the weapon and swung it at the zombie, destroying another beast. She slammed into another zombie but was flustered when an arrow flew through the door and sliced her unarmored arm.

"Ouch!" she cried as she stared at group of skeletons charging toward the house. "This is all my fault," she hollered. "I'm sorry."

"Your fault? How can you say that?" Billy was shocked that Dina blamed herself. This wasn't her fault. She had the right to deny the traveler her mooshrooms.

"You aren't to blame," Amira said as she slammed her sword into another zombie.

Anna, Peyton, Erin, and Edison sprinted toward the skeletons and fought with their swords and potions. When Allyson, Billy, Amira, and Dina annihilated the remaining zombies, they bolted outside to help the gang battle the bony beasts. Dina banged her sword against a bony skeletons. It took a few hits, but soon she destroyed a skeleton.

"You're a born warrior," said Anna.

Dina had spent her entire life on Mushroom Island because she was terrified of battling hostile mobs, but now she regretted not traveling. She told herself that once the curse was lifted, she would travel around the Overworld and explore every biome.

The skeletons were annihilated, and the gang began

to spout out various plans for stopping the curse. They all spoke at once, and nobody was listening to anyone else.

Edison called out, "Stop!"

Anna said, "Yes, I know we all have good plans and the same common goal of stopping the traveler who put a curse on the Island, but we also have to let each of our voices be heard."

There wasn't any time for people's voices to be heard, because as Anna tried to create order amongst the group, there was an explosion and another creepy loud noise.

"The Wither!" Anna cried.

A flying, three-headed Wither changed from blue to black as it spit wither skulls from its trio of mouths. One of the smoky projectiles struck Dina, and she froze as her heart turned black. She was struck with the Wither effect. She couldn't speak. Unable to move her arms, she dropped her sword on the ground. Edison sprinted over to her and gave her a sip of milk. He said, "This will stop the Wither effect."

Dina barely had enough energy to sip the milk, but once she was able to swallow the milk, her energy returned. She picked up her sword and asked, "How do we destroy this?"

"Watch out!" Anna warned Dina, but it was too late. She was struck with the Wither effect again, and Edison gave her the last sip of milk from his inventory.

"You have to shield yourself from the wither skulls, because I'm out of milk," Edison told her.

Anna handed Dina a bow and arrow and informed her, "This is easier."

Dina stood in her doorway as she sent arrows at the three-headed beast. She hit its belly, and the Wither lost a heart, but it was still strong. Anna and Amira shot a barrage of arrows that hit the Wither, diminishing its health, but the Wither sprouted armor and was now immune to arrows.

Dina marveled as the beast put on armor. "This is a tricky beast," she remarked.

The Wither flew closer to the ground, and Edison hurtled toward the armored beast, splashing potions on the Wither and weakening it. The Wither shot a wither skull at him, striking Edison with the Wither effect.

"Help me!" His voice was low.

Edison was shocked when he saw Omar appear and rush toward him with a bottle of milk.

"Sip this, my friend," Omar said as Edison regained his strength from the milk.

As Edison finished the milk, Omar splashed potion on the Wither, destroying it and forcing it to drop a Nether star. Omar reached down and placed the Nether star in his inventory. Edison was glad Omar came to his rescue, but he was concerned that Omar had taken the Nether star. One could use the Nether star to craft a beacon. A beacon had the power to harm everyone on the Island. Edison hoped Omar wasn't planning on doing anything bad. He told himself that Omar had saved him and destroyed the Wither, and maybe he shouldn't be suspicious of his old friend.

"Thank you for helping me," said Edison.

The gang ran through the dark and surrounded Omar. They congratulated him for destroying the Wither.

"Great job," said Allyson.

Dina introduced herself to Omar. He smiled. "It's nice to meet you, Lina."

"It's Dina," she corrected him.

Edison realized that there was something still off with Omar, but he wondered if it was related to some unknown illness or glitch, and perhaps it wasn't as sinister as they had originally thought. But he was still suspicious when Omar said, "I'm sorry. Nice meeting you Dina," and began to cough.

10
DOPPELGANGERS

The sun came up and Anna smiled. "At least we have a break from hostile mobs for a little while."

"We should head into town and start questioning the townspeople," suggested Allyson. "I know most of them."

"So do I," said Dina. "That's a good idea."

"Is this about the curse you were telling me about?" asked Omar.

"Yes." Allyson blurted out the whole story about Dina and the traveler who wanted her mooshrooms in one breath. The entire time she spoke, Edison wanted to interrupt her and point out that Omar had a cough and he could be the person behind the curse, but instead he stood by silently and watched Omar's reaction.

"We have to stop this," said Omar. "This is awful. The people of Mushroom Island aren't prepared for a battle. Also, we were here to celebrate Amira's birthday, and we have to find time to enjoy ourselves. We have to stop the curse."

Edison was surprised that Omar was so concerned about the curse. This wasn't the reaction Edison had expected.

Everyone agreed that they had to stop the curse, but the only plan they had was to question the merchants in town. As they raced toward the blacksmith's shop, he emerged and started shouting. His green eyes focused on Omar. "You are a thief!"

"What?" questioned Omar.

"This man came into my blacksmith shop and stole from me. He told me he would trade two emeralds for armor, but as I handed him the armor, he escaped out of my shop."

"I didn't do that!" Omar exclaimed.

"No, I know it's you," declared the blacksmith.

"You have the wrong—" Omar screamed as he coughed, "—person."

"Really?" questioned the blacksmith.

"Yes, I've never been in the town. I went to the festival and then I got lost trying to get to a friend's house. I haven't been feeling well," explained Omar.

"Well, you must have a twin on this island," explained the blacksmith.

Allyson said, "I think you have confused our friend Omar with someone else. We are all here because we're trying to stop the curse that's been placed on Mushroom Island."

"The curse." The blacksmith laughed.

"What's so funny about a curse?" asked Amira.

"I can't believe people really believe that a curse is behind this," he replied, "when we all know someone is trying to distract us as they steal all of the mooshrooms."

"Steal all of the mooshrooms?" asked Allyson.

"Yes," said the blacksmith. "Look around the Island. There are no mooshrooms left. Our entire island has been robbed of mooshrooms."

"What?" Allyson was shocked. "I can't believe it."

The white-robed librarian raced from the library and called out, "Isn't it terrible? All of the mooshrooms are missing."

"They're not missing," said the blacksmith, "They've been stolen."

"I knew the mooshroom festival was a bad idea. Last year we had a similar incident, although it was much smaller," remarked the librarian.

"What happened last year?" questioned Anna.

"Someone stole from a farm. They took two mooshrooms. This year, all of the mooshrooms are gone." Tears filled the librarian's eyes.

Edison asked, "Do you happen to know who might be behind all of this?"

The librarian paused. "It's odd, but there was a man who looked like your friend over there. He stole a book from the library. I thought he was suspicious." She pointed to Omar.

Omar raised his hands in the air. "I promise, I didn't do anything." He started to cough again.

Dina remarked, "The person who tried to steal from and placed a curse on me also had a cough."

Omar defended himself. "You can't think that everyone who has a cough is the person who cursed you, can you?"

"Well," Dina said and looked down at the ground. She didn't have a response.

"Do I look like the person who cursed you?" asked Omar.

"No, you don't."

"I don't understand why everyone is placing blame on me. I haven't done anything wrong, I promise." Omar was upset.

A voice called out, "Guys, I've been looking all over for you." Greta rushed down the grassy main street. Her violet hair waved in the wind.

"Greta," said Allyson, "have you seen any mooshrooms?" Allyson couldn't believe all of the mooshrooms had been removed from the island, and she needed confirmation.

"No," Greta replied, "there aren't any mooshrooms on the island. Haven't you heard? They've all been stolen."

"You didn't believe me?" the blacksmith raised his voice.

"I did," said Allyson. "I just couldn't believe it. It seems so crazy. I was hoping Greta had seen one mooshroom. The idea that our island doesn't have one roaming in the pasture is upsetting."

"It's upsetting to everyone," said Greta, and then she paused as she focused on Omar. "I just saw you."

"What?" Omar asked. "Me?"

"Yes," she said. "I just saw you."

"Where?" he asked.

"On the way here," she said. "I walked past you a minute ago."

"I think you have a twin," the blacksmith said as he stared at Omar.

"There is more than one of me? That's nuts," said Omar.

Edison suggested, "Maybe somebody stole your skin or made a duplicate of it?"

Omar questioned, "Who would do that?"

"I don't know," said Anna, "but someone was trying to attack you in Verdant Valley the other night, and I think they're behind this."

"I think we should go back to Verdant Valley and investigate," suggested Edison.

"Whoever was bothering him there is obviously on this island," said Anna.

Edison wondered if the Omar they were with was the innocent one or if he was the Omar that was behind the chaos.

11

NO UMBRELLAS HERE

Omar asked Greta, "Can you lead me to the person who looked like me? Where did you see him?"

"Of course," she replied. "I saw your twin at a farm right outside of town."

"Finally, we'll be able to clear this up." Omar instructed Greta to lead them to the person who she thought was his twin.

They were hurrying toward the farm when a thunderous noise shook the grassy island.

"Oh no!" cried Dina. "Another explosion."

Smoke rose in the distance. Dina and Allyson ran toward the smoke, but Omar called out, "What about the farm? I need to find this person who is impersonating me."

"We have to help these people," cried Dina.

Omar reluctantly followed the gang toward the

smoke and away from the farm. When they reached the site of the explosion, they let out a collective gasp when they saw a gaping hole in the ground.

"What was here?" Edison asked as he looked at the rubble, trying to decipher what had stood in that spot.

Tears filled Dina's eyes as she spoke. "This is my friend Louis's farm. I have no idea where he is. I hope he's okay."

Dina walked them past the burning remnants of the farmhouse and toward the pasture, where she pointed out, "This is where he kept his mooshrooms. They're all gone. I can't believe there aren't any mooshrooms on the island. It seems unreal. I feel like this entire attack on Mushroom Island is my fault."

"You can't say things like that, because it's not true," said Allyson. "This person or these people are attacking our island. You had every right not to give up your mooshrooms. I don't ever want to hear you blame yourself again."

"I wish there was something I could do to stop this," said Dina.

Billy declared, "We will stop this. For the last year Anna, Edison, and I have been stopping all sorts of problems that have occurred in the Overworld, and we will stop this too."

Edison hoped Billy was right, but there was no time to ponder this thought because the sky grew dark and thunder shook the ground. Heavy rain poured down on them, and a sea of skeletons spawned in front of them. The skeletons unleashed a barrage of arrows that pierced through their unarmored limbs, weakening the group.

Four creepers spawned behind the skeletons. Edison struck one with an arrow, destroying the explosive mob. Another was destroyed by a skeleton's arrow, and it dropped a music disc. Edison had never seen this before and risked being destroyed and respawning in Farmer's Bay to grab the music disc.

"Are you nuts?" Billy asked him.

"No." He carefully placed the disc in his inventory. "When this is all over, we're going to have a big party for Amira's birthday, and we'll play this."

Amira screamed as she battled the skeletons alongside her friends. "Thanks, but stop talking and fight!"

A creeper exploded and destroyed Greta as the gang tried to battle the creepers that invaded the landscape. Edison skillfully destroyed a creeper as he watched a bolt of lightning strike the remaining creeper, creating a rare charged creeper.

"Stand back!" Billy warned his friend. "The charged creeper is incredibly powerful."

Edison tried to flee from the creeper while aiming his bow and arrow at the green beast wearing a dark frown, but he couldn't escape. The last thing he heard and saw were a deafening explosion and a flash of light, and he woke up to the sound of Puddles meowing.

Edison looked out the window. Everything was eerily calm in Farmer's Bay. If they hadn't left for Amira's birthday celebration on Mushroom Island, they would have no indication that something was going on there.

The world seemed peaceful. The farm was luscious, and the sun was shining. A few people walked down the sandy path toward the beach without a care in the world. Edison wished he could be as calm as the two beachgoers, but he was too worried about his friends. He had to make his way back to Mushroom Island. He TPed to them and landed in the center of the battle.

"Watch out!" Billy screamed as arrows flew past Edison.

Edison grabbed his sword from his inventory and leaped at a skeleton. The creepers were gone, but there were more skeletons.

"They keep spawning," Anna said breathlessly. "Even with all of our manpower, we can't seem to defeat them."

Edison joined his friends in battle. He annihilated two skeletons and tried to destroy another, then spotted a person off in the distance who wore the same black jacket as Omar.

"I think it's your doppleganger!" he called out to Omar.

"Where?" Omar asked as a skeleton's arrow sliced into his arm and destroyed his last heart. He vanished.

12
REUNITED

"Omar!" Amira cried.

The gang was shocked when Omar's doppelganger sprinted toward them and called out, "Guys, I thought I'd never find you."

Edison almost dropped his bow and arrow, but he was jolted back to battle when a skeleton's arrow scratched his arm. He quickly shot an arrow at the skeleton, but it never reached the bony beast because the sun came up and the hostile mobs disappeared. The battle was over, and the gang was standing next to the rubble of Louis's farm as Omar said, "You have no idea how hard it was to find you guys. I missed the boat because I was being held prisoner, and then I tried to TP here, but I've been dealing with a bunch of odd glitches."

"Where were you held prisoner?" asked Anna.

"Didn't you guys hear me calling for help when we were in Verdant Valley?" asked Omar.

"Yes," said Edison, "but when I respawned that night, you were in my bungalow going through my potions."

"No, I wasn't," he said. "What are you talking about?"

Anna clarified, "So this is the first time you've seen us since I saw you in Verdant Valley?"

"Yes," Omar replied.

"But we've seen you," said Amira.

"What?" Omar questioned his friends.

Peyton and Erin spoke at once. They tried to explain what had happened and how Omar had traveled with them to Mushroom Island.

"And you had a cough," said Peyton.

"A cough?" questioned Omar.

"Yeah, you kept coughing," confirmed Erin.

Dina exclaimed, "I knew it! That man dressed in your friend's skin was the traveler who cursed me."

"What curse?" Omar didn't know anything about the curse, and as he heard the story, Edison watched his reactions. He knew this was the real Omar. What he didn't know was who was underneath the other Omar's skin. They had to expose this criminal.

Omar asked, "Why would someone want to impersonate me?"

"I don't know," said Anna, "but we will find out."

"Who kept you prisoner?" asked Billy. "I think once we figure out that part of the story, we will find our answers."

Omar wasn't very helpful. He didn't know who had kept him prisoner. "I was leaving the castle and a man approached me about a building project. I told him that I didn't have time to work on it at the moment, but I would in a month. This irritated him, and he told me that I was his prisoner and I must work on the project right now."

"Wow," exclaimed Anna. "And then what did he do?"

"I told him that I refused to be his prisoner, but as I spoke, he splashed me with a potion of Weakness, and I could barely move. He forced me into a minecart and then took me to a cave between Verdant Valley and Farmer's Bay. I had one heart left, and I had no energy to fight back. It was nighttime, and he crafted a bed in the cave. I slept there under his watch. A large cave spider crawled toward me and I knew that if I were bitten, I'd be destroyed. I hoped this man didn't see the spider, because I wanted to respawn in my bed in the castle, but he saw it and destroyed it. Then he forced me to eat an apple so I'd have enough energy to survive another day. I don't think he expected the hostile mob attack, and he was upset that he was distracted by a creeper that spawned in the cave, and I was able to escape to the front of the tunnel to call for help."

"That's when we heard you," said Anna.

"Yes, I could hear you and Edison calling my name, but that just infuriated this man, and he struck me with a sword, which left me with one heart. Then he walked me to the back of the cave, where there was a stronghold, and then put me in a jail. It took me two days to escape, and then I just TPed here."

"Didn't you see us with the other Omar?" asked Amira.

"No," he said. "But why there is somebody walking around with my skin?"

"I assume it's the same person who kept you as a prisoner," said Billy.

"But why would he do this?" asked Omar. "I never did anything wrong. I was just working on the castle."

Dina introduced herself. "I'm Dina, and I had a similar situation as you. I was just working on my farm when someone who wanted my mooshrooms approached me. When I refused to give them to him, he put a curse on the island. Now our peaceful island is being attacked by all sorts of hostile mobs."

"That's terrible," he said.

"Is there anything you can remember about this person?" asked Anna.

"He wore ripped jeans and a blue shirt. His hair was yellow, and he had glasses," he said.

"Anything else?" questioned Peyton.

"He had a cough," said Omar, "which I thought was strange. Sometimes he had trouble speaking."

Dina said, "That's the same man who cursed the island."

"And I think we accidently brought him with us to Mushroom Island," said Amira.

"What?" questioned Omar.

"We thought he was you," said Amira.

Edison wanted it put on the record that he never thought it was Omar, but he kept quiet.

"Where is he now?" asked Omar.

"We have to find him," said Anna.

Edison said, "If he slept when you were in the cave, that means he must be there."

"Should we go back there, or do you think we should wait for him to return?" questioned Peyton.

"We have to TP back to Verdant Valley," suggested Anna.

"Yes," said Edison. "We will surprise him there."

"I've never left Mushroom Island," Dina confessed. "I don't even know how to TP."

"We'll show you," said Anna. "You've fought so many mobs that you're prepared now."

"I don't think we have to go anywhere," said Allyson.

"Why not?" asked Dina.

"Look over there," Allyson said as she pointed to the man dressed in Omar's skin. He was in the distance crafting a portal to the Nether.

13

NETHER SAID THAT

Purple smoke surrounded the imposter as he disappeared in front of their eyes. Edison lunged toward the portal and hopped on without turning around to see if his friends had joined him. He emerged in the fiery Nether, clutching his bow and arrow as he looked in the sky for any ghasts or blazes that might want to attack him. His friends hadn't spawned right behind him like he assumed they would.

He also didn't see the imposter. Edison climbed to the top of a large netherrack platform that overlooked a lava waterfall. He could see a Nether fortress off in the distance, but he didn't see the imposter or his friends. He didn't want to travel to the Nether fortress on his own, and he considered crafting a portal back to Mushroom Island. Edison climbed down the ladder on the platform and walked toward the spot where he spawned in the Nether. Two zombie pigmen walked by him, but he didn't lock eyes with them, and they ignored him.

Edison was searching through his inventory for the resources he needed to build a portal when he heard a familiar voice call out, "Edison!"

He looked up to see Billy, Anna, and all of his other friends rushing toward him. Edison also saw three ghasts flying behind them. He called out to his friends, warning them about the mobs, but it was too late. Amira was struck by one of the fireballs that the ghast shot at her. It landed on her back, and by the time she turned around, she was pelted by two more fireballs and disappeared.

Edison shot an arrow at the ghasts, instantly destroying one of the white, blocky creatures with tentacles. Dina was frozen. She had never seen a ghast and wasn't sure what to do. Edison called out, "Dina, stay away from the fireballs. If they come toward you, use your fist to deflect it."

"What?" Dina looked down at her hand. She couldn't imagine how painful touching a ghast might be, and she worried she'd get burned. Dina pulled a bow and arrow from her inventory. She ran toward Edison and shot arrows alongside him. One of the arrows hit a ghast and destroyed it.

"You're a quick learner," Anna called out as she watched Dina destroy another ghast.

When the gang destroyed the ghasts, Edison told them about the Nether fortress in the distance. "Should we go there? Do you think the imposter Omar might be hiding there?"

"We should head in that direction," said Anna. "I don't want to lose sight of our goal. I know there's a lot of treasure to be found in a Nether fortress, but we have to think about Mushroom Island. They are being destroyed, and we have to get back there to help them."

Everyone agreed this was the best plan. Edison did need some Nether wart, but he didn't want to mention the possibility of picking some up in the Nether fortress. He hoped he could find a minute to gather some, but he knew that they had to be focused or they might not be able to capture this menace.

"What type of hostile mobs spawn at night?" questioned Dina.

"There is no night in the Nether," explained Anna.

"What? It's daylight all the time?" asked Dina.

"I don't know if you'd call this daylight," said Peyton, "but it's always the same in the Nether."

"I'm not a fan of the Nether," confessed Edison.

"I don't think anybody likes the Nether," said Billy. "I should say that I like the treasures and resources I can get here, but it's certainly not my favorite place to be. It's very dangerous."

Dina stopped along the lava river. "If we touch the lava, we can be destroyed, right?"

"Yes," warned Erin. "Stay away from the lava."

Dina knew the Nether wasn't the most hospitable environment, but she was in awe of it. There was something quite beautiful about the color of lava. When they approached the Nether fortress, she said, "This is such a gorgeous place."

"Watch out!" Billy called out as a group of blazes rose from the ground ready to attack anybody who wanted to enter the fortress. One of the yellow creatures locked eyes with the group. One of the were the protectors of the fortress and didn't want just anybody to enter. If you had the skills to defeat these fiery, yellow multi-limbed mobs, then you deserved admission to the fortress.

Dina had no idea how to destroy a blaze, but she could spend an entire day staring at it. She thought it was just as pretty as her mooshrooms. When she thought of her mooshrooms, she remembered what was happening on Mushroom Island, and that's when she took out her bow and arrow and shot at the blaze. She couldn't be distracted. She had to stop this person who had cursed Mushroom Island. She had to find out if he was in the Nether fortress.

The final blaze was destroyed, and the gang walked through the doors into a large room with a staircase. Edison eyed the Nether wart growing next to a patch of soul sand.

"You should pick it up," said Billy. "We'll look around for the imposter."

There wasn't time to pick up the Nether wart, because as Edison grabbed some, he heard Allyson scream, "He's here!"

The gang rushed down a long corridor and into a small room where they saw three people who looked like Omar. Omar hollered at them, "Who are you?" The trio laughed and splashed a potion of Invisibility and disappeared.

"Where did they go?" screamed Omar.

"You'll never find us," one of the Omars called out, but they could only follow the sound of his voice, and they lost him.

"Should we go back to Mushroom Island or stay here?" asked Dina.

"We have to find them," said Allyson.

The gang scrambled through the hot Nether. Sweat fell from their faces and got into their eyes, clouding their vision, as they traveled farther away from the fortress.

Dina asked if they could stop so she could catch her breath. "Where do you think the three Omars are headed? I feel like we're running without a plan."

"Can we not refer to them by my name?" asked Omar. "I don't have anything to do with them, and I have no idea why they want to walk around in the same black jacket that I wear and with my face. They should use their own skins."

"They're cowards," said Anna. "If they weren't, they'd be able to show their own faces."

As they spoke, Allyson spotted three people off in the distance. They were in the midst of a battle with two zombie pigmen.

"Is that them?" asked Allyson.

"I think so!" said Dina, and they sprinted toward the trio that struggled to defeat a couple of zombie pigmen.

14
HOME AGAIN

Despite putting up a tough fight, the trio defeated the zombie pigmen and then hopped on a portal and vanished in a purple haze. The gang jumped on the portal after them. Standing close together, Edison said, "I hope this winds up in Mushroom Island."

"I do too," said Allyson.

When they emerged, it was a familiar landscape, but it wasn't Mushroom Island. They were in Verdant Valley.

Omar suggested, "We should go to the cave where he kept me prisoner. I bet that's where they are staying."

The group hurried out of Verdant Valley and toward the cave. They grabbed torches from their inventories as they walked into the musty cave, and Edison led them to the back and opened the door to a stronghold.

"We have to be careful," said Omar. "We don't want them to trap us."

Omar walked through the door, and someone sliced into his arm with a diamond sword.

Edison gasped when he saw twenty people dressed like Omar in the small stronghold. They all carried diamond swords, and they leaped at the gang. Omar was lost in the group, and Edison couldn't tell which was Omar and which were imposters.

Edison screamed to his friends, "We have to get out of here."

"We can't leave Omar," cried Anna.

"There is no way we can battle these imposters in the stronghold," said Edison.

"We have no other option, and we can't talk about it," said Anna as she slammed her diamond sword into a person she hoped wasn't Omar.

Edison pulled potions from his inventory and splashed them on the many Omars and called out, "Please leave the real Omar alone."

Laughter erupted from the army of Omars as they attacked the group. Billy cried for help when four Omars surrounded him and he was unable to break free. He was losing hearts quickly and would be destroyed within a couple of strikes.

Using his sword, Edison slew two of the Omars and splashed potions on the other two. Anna rushed to their sides and annihilated the remaining Omars that threatened Billy. Edison handed Billy a potion to regain strength as he slammed his sword into another Omar.

"This is intense," said Billy.

"I keep thinking that I'm destroying Omar," confessed Anna.

"I think we'll know the real Omar when we see him," said Billy.

"I hope so," Anna replied as she swung her sword at a man who looked just like her good friend Omar. She told herself that it wasn't him.

Edison heard the real Omar's cries from deep within the stronghold, "I hear him, don't you?" he asked Billy and Anna, who fought by his side.

"Yes!" Anna exclaimed. "But how are we going to get to him?"

"We will just have to fight our way through this crowd," he said as he splashed potions and used his sword to weave through a crowd of hostile people in dressed in fake skins.

Dina screamed out from the other side of the stronghold. She was overwhelmed by the attack. Edison wanted to help her, but he saw Allyson, Peyton, and Erin dash to her side, which alleviated his guilt.

As Edison, Billy, and Anna tried to find their way to the real Omar, they could see a cluster of skeletons in a dimly lit section of the stronghold. "Do you think they know skeletons are spawning down here?" asked Edison.

"I don't know, but they can only help us," said Billy.

"Yes," said Anna. "If we avoid the skeletons, they can attack these fake Omars."

The gang narrowly avoided getting destroyed by the skeletons as they saw Omar being placed in a jail cell in the stronghold. "That's probably where they kept him the last time."

"I wonder which one is the leader of the group?" asked Anna. "It's hard to tell when they're all wearing the same skin."

They sprinted toward the jail cell, but there were two people who looked like Omar guarding the dirty jail cell that housed their friend.

"Omar," Edison called out, "we're going to get you out of here."

"Don't waste your time trying to break me out of here." Omar's voice was weak.

"We have to save you," said Edison as he lunged at the guard.

Billy and Anna ripped into the second guard with their diamond swords, and he was destroyed. They helped Edison defeat the remaining guard as Omar said, "There is someone who is the head of all of this, but he's not here."

"Where is he?" asked Edison as he tried to open the locked gate. He slammed his sword against the bars, but they were stuck.

"He's on Mushroom Island," Omar's voice was even fainter than before.

"How many hearts do you have left?" asked Anna as she handed Omar a potion to regain his strength. It was hard to get it through the slots of the bars, and some of the potion spilled on the dirt ground.

Omar barely had the strength to sip the potion, but once he did, he felt a lot stronger and more hopeful. He had to tell his friends about his discovery. Once he told them, they'd be on the brink of stopping the person behind these attacks and solving the case.

Omar took his last sip and was finally able to talk. Anna asked, "Feel better?"

"Yes, but I have something to tell you," he said quickly. "I overheard two of these guys talking. There is someone behind this, and he's stolen Amira's boat and is transporting the mooshrooms from the island."

"To where?" asked Anna.

"I don't know where," said Omar, "but we have to stop him."

Edison felt a sword slice into his arm, and an arrow hit his leg. The pain radiated throughout his body. He awoke in his bed, and his body still hurt.

He looked out the window. He wanted to TP back to his friends, but it was dark out, and he heard rattling outside his door. He sipped a potion of Strength, took a bite of an apple, and readjusted his armor. He had to be prepared. Once they rescued Omar, they were going to be in for a long night.

As he readied himself to TP to the cave, he heard a familiar sound outside his window. It called out, "Moo."

15
ON THE SHORE

Edison's door was ripped off its hinges, and he was face to face with four zombies. He knew the potions and the sword were powerful, but he was only one person, and battling them would be very tough. The zombie's odor overwhelmed him as he grabbed another bottle of potion from his inventory and soaked the zombie that grabbed his arm. There was nobody there to help him, and despite destroying one zombie and weakening the others, the zombies annihilated him and Edison awoke in his bed. He looked up, and the zombies were gone.

"Edison," Billy called out as he raced into Edison's living room, "are you here?"

"Yes," Edison replied, and he got up from his bed. He was wobbly and pulled a potion from his inventory to regain his strength. "I need to get more milk," he told Billy.

Billy pulled a bottle from his inventory. "Keep this. You don't look well."

"Thank you, I'm okay," he said. "I was just overwhelmed during a zombie battle."

Amira rushed through the door, "Did you see the mooshrooms?" she asked them.

"Amira, you're here!" Billy smiled. "When you were destroyed in the Nether I wasn't sure if you were on Mushroom Island."

"I came here because I tracked my boat to this shore. The person who is behind this has stolen all of the mooshrooms and left them at Farmer's Bay. There is hardly room to move, there are so many mooshrooms roaming about. There are some bathing on the shore. The strange thing is they just abandoned the mooshrooms. It seems like the only plan they had was removing them from Mushroom Island. They don't seem to have any idea what to do with them afterward."

"That is weird," said Billy.

The door had been ripped from its hinges, and as the sun came up a mooshroom peeked its head through the narrow doorway and let out a loud *moo*.

"What are we going to do with all of these mooshrooms?" asked Billy. "They're probably destroying our town's farm."

Edison was craving a bowl of mooshroom stew, but he didn't admit this. It wasn't a time to eat. He had to find his other friends. He wondered if the people who stole the mooshrooms captured them.

"How did you get out of the stronghold?" Edison asked Billy.

"Stronghold? Where's the stronghold?" questioned Amira.

"I was destroyed a few minutes after you," explained Billy. "I think we should TP there to see if Omar and the others are okay."

Billy and Edison told Amira about the stronghold filled with numerous Omars and she gasped, "How are we going to find the real Omar?"

"I don't think the real Omar is in that stronghold. We have to stop whoever is behind this attack," said Edison, and they TPed to the stronghold.

When they spawned in the stronghold, the only person left was Anna. She was in the jail. Her health bar was incredibly low. She tried to call out to them, but her voice was too weak. "Guys," she said, but then stopped. She didn't have the energy to speak.

"Anna." Edison darted to the jail and slipped the milk between the slots. "Drink this, and we'll get you out of here."

She took a large gulp. "The Omars have Peyton, Erin, Allyson, and Dina. I don't know where they took them. I was trying to fight one of them, and they tossed me in this jail. I had to watch as our friends were taken off to another location, and I couldn't help them at all." Tears filled Anna's eyes as she spoke.

Amira tried to open the prison gate, but it wasn't easy. She slammed her sword against the bolt. Then a voice called out, "Edison, Anna, Billy!"

They turned around to see Omar carrying a torch. He walked toward them.

"Stay back," Edison said as he pointed his diamond sword at Omar.

"What are you doing? It's me, Omar," he explained.

"We've seen a lot of you," said Billy.

"I know, but it's really me," proclaimed Omar.

"How can we be sure it's really you?" asked Billy.

"I know," said Amira. "We traveled together for a long time, and there are many things only both of us know. Remember when we were returning treasures. What was the first place we docked?"

"On the shore of an ice-cold biome. Our boat almost got stuck in the ice," said Omar.

"That's true," said Amira. "You are the real Omar."

Omar rushed over to them and helped break Anna out of the jail, but when they sprinted toward the exit, Omar let out a loud gasp.

The army of Omars crowded the exit. They all clutched bows and arrows and aimed at the group.

One of the Omars shouted, "Fire," and the gang was destroyed.

16

DISCOVERIES

Edison awoke in his bed to the sounds of mooshrooms mooing outside his window. There was a noise coming from his living room. It sounded like footsteps.

"Billy?" he called out, but there was no response. Edison adjusted his armor and pulled a diamond sword from his inventory as he walked into the living room, ready to defend himself from the unknown person who was in house.

As Edison leaped out of his bedroom with his sword, a voice called out, "Edison! It's me, Omar!"

Edison wasn't sure it was the real Omar. He decided he'd put him to the test, like Amira, and ask him questions that only the real Omar would know. But he didn't have a chance. Another Omar zipped through the door and screamed, "Imposter!" Their diamond swords clanged as they battled each other.

Edison stood in awe as two more Omars entered the bungalow and started to battle. He wanted to sprint past the two sets of battling Omars and run to Billy's house to explain what was happening in his living room. Instead, he just watched as Puddles brushed up against his legs and meowed. He hoped he'd discover clues as he watched them fight, but there were no words spoken, just a battle. He wished he knew if one of these Omars was the real one.

"Moo." Another mooshroom popped its head through the doorway, but it couldn't fit inside the living room.

Edison could see Billy, Amira, and Anna outside of his window. He called out to them, "Please come in here!"

The trio sprinted into his living room and paused when they saw the chaos. One of the Omars had been destroyed, and there were three left battling each other.

"Why are you fighting each other?" asked Anna.

The Omars stopped, "We must all be destroyed."

"That doesn't make any sense," said Amira.

"We were told to destroy anybody who looks like us," one of the Omars breathlessly explained.

"Why? Who told you to do that?" asked Anna.

"We can't tell you," said an Omar.

The three Omars continued fighting when one more was annihilated.

"What happens when there's only one left?" asked Anna.

She didn't have time to hear a response. Within a second, there was one Omar standing in front of her.

He leaped at Anna and plunged his sword into her unarmored arm.

Her first instinct was to fight back, but she didn't want to destroy this Omar. She wanted to interrogate him and find out who was behind all of these attacks.

Edison splashed a potion of Strength on the Omar, which irritated him. "Why would you do that?"

"We will make sure you stay alive forever," said Edison.

"Tell us who is behind these attacks," Amira demanded.

"Never!" he replied as he struck Amira with his diamond sword.

The sounds of mooshrooms grew louder, and Anna asked, "Why did they bring all of the mooshrooms to Farmer's Bay?"

Omar didn't respond. He kept battling them, but they wouldn't strike him. Instead they shot a series of questions at him.

"Why are you doing this?"

"What is your plan for the mooshrooms?"

"Can't you see what you're doing to the Overworld?"

This Omar didn't say a word. He didn't even react until Peyton, Erin, Allyson and Dina exploded through the door with another Omar. The silent Omar sprinted toward the new Omar and began to swipe him with his sword.

"Leave him alone. We know your story. Your gang is over, and you are done terrorizing the Overworld," screamed Allyson.

"Never!" he hollered and struck the Omar who just walked through the door.

Allyson hit him with her diamond sword, but Edison told her that she shouldn't destroy this imposter Omar, because he might have answers.

"I told you guys," Allyson said as she destroyed the Omar, "we have the answers."

"Tell us what you know," said Anna.

Allyson explained, "We just escaped from the boat where we were held prisoner."

Erin said, "We overheard the leader talking. He has made an error, which is why the mooshrooms are here. The boat is broken, and he's trying to fix it. He thinks the weight from all of the mooshrooms was too much for the boat. When he unloaded a couple, they all escaped. He has no idea how to get them back."

"Why does he want the mooshrooms?" asked Edison.

Erin said, "His big plan was to steal all the mooshrooms and then deliver them to people across the Overworld. He thought he'd be able to have a lot of great trades because they're so rare."

"So there was never really a curse?" asked Amira.

"No, just a criminal. The same one who approached Dina," said Allyson.

"Yes, we saw him without his Omar skin. It was the same guy," confirmed Dina.

"How are we going to stop him?" asked Edison.

"We have a plan," the real Omar said with a smile.

17
MOOSHROOMS

"What's the plan?" asked Edison.

"Since I look like them, I'm going to make them believe I'm in their army. I'm going to start returning the mooshrooms to the boat. Amira, you should fix the boat, and we should all travel back to Mushroom Island. The leader will follow us back there, and we'll capture him," explained Omar.

"That sounds too easy," said Anna.

"Easy?" questioned Omar. "I think it's going to be one of the hardest things we've ever done."

The gang followed Omar outside and helped him lead the mooshrooms back on the ship, but only three mooshrooms fit on the small boat. "How did he transport all of these mooshrooms on this boat?" questioned Amira. "No wonder it broke," she remarked while attempting to fix the boat. There was a large hole on the bottom, and she pulled a wooden plank from her inventory and placed it over the hole.

One of the Omars saw them place the mooshrooms on the ship. "What are you doing? The mooshrooms stay here."

The real Omar made his way to the front of the ship. "No, there has been a change of plans. He wants us to build boats and bring the mooshrooms back to Mushroom Island."

"I never heard about that plan," said the Omar lookalike.

"Well, it's true," said Omar. "Call the others over and help us build ships."

"Who are these people that are helping you?" asked the man.

"They are my prisoners. Once we get to Mushroom Island, I am to construct a prison and leave them in there."

The other Omar seemed satisfied with this response and called over a few more soldiers. They stood on the shores of Farmer's Bay crafting boats. When one boat was done, they would lead a group of mooshrooms onto the ship. Once the ship was full, Omar instructed them to set sail to Mushroom Island.

The first boat filled with mooshrooms took off for Mushroom Island when a gang of Omars approached and questioned them.

"This isn't what we are supposed to be doing," a fake Omar argued.

"Yes," Omar said, "it is. We have to bring the mooshrooms back to Mushroom Island."

"That's not the plan. I'm going to report you," said the fake Omar.

"Let's go!" said Omar."I want to be there when you report me."

"It's my pleasure," said the fake Omar as he marched away from the shore of Farmer's Bay and to the cave near Verdant Valley. But he stopped when he saw Omar was not alone. "You can't bring them in here."

"But they're my prisoners." He pointed to Allyson, Dina, Erin, Peyton, Amira, Anna, Edison, and Billy. "I can't let them go. Also, he'll be happy to see them. He knows they have been trying to stop him."

"I don't trust them, and I don't trust you," the fake Omar hollered, and he called for backup. As he screamed, a seemingly neverending stream of Omars sprinted from the cave and shot arrows. The Omars leaped toward the gang with their diamond swords.

Edison's hearts were depleting quickly, and he tried to grab a potion from his inventory to regain his strength, but it was impossible. Another Omar struck his leg while another shot a stream of arrows at his arm. He was weak and in pain, and he let out an agonized cry. He knew this was the end and that he'd be destroyed and would respawn in his home, but he wanted to help his friends.

"Edison." Dina handed him a potion of Strength. "Drink this," she said as she slew the two Omars who had attacked Edison. He regained his energy and stood beside Dina as they battled the army of Omars.

The real Omar wanted to find out who was

orchestrating this plot against Mushroom Island and who had also stolen his skin. He wove his way through the crowd of lookalikes and spotted an Omar standing in the back of cave ordering the soldiers to leave.

Omar tore toward him with his diamond sword. He pointed and demanded, "Change your skin."

"It's really you." He laughed and then let out a cough.

"Yes, I am the real Omar. Now, I don't know why you chose to create an army of soldiers who look like me or why you choose to wear my skin, but it has to stop. This is over."

"Over?" He laughed again, and his cough grew stronger. "This is just the beginning."

"The beginning?" Omar pierced the other man's leg with the diamond sword.

This infuriated the leader. "Don't ever strike me again," he said as he swiftly pulled a potion from his inventory and splashed it on Omar.

Omar was down to two hearts. He called for help, but his friends couldn't hear him. They were too busy battling the army outside of the cave. The leader said, "Nobody is going to help you. It's time to give up. Soon I will be selling my mooshrooms all over the universe, and I'll be the richest person in the Overworld. When I am rich, I will have power." He laughed and coughed at the same time.

Omar pulled a potion from his inventory, splashed it on himself, and became invisible. He sprinted through the cave and to his friends. He needed backup.

He had to defeat this criminal. When he emerged from the cave, he was thrown down as an explosion rocked the ground. The cave exploded.

"What's happening?" screamed a soldier.

Edison sprinted toward Omar, making this way through the smoke. "Are you okay?"

"Yes, but the leader was in there," said Omar.

Two soldiers came over to Omar. They changed skins in front of him, Transforming from Omar, with his jet-black hair and black jacket, to their own skins. One had flaming red hair, and the other had purple hair and wore glasses.

"It's over," the soldier with the purple hair told him. "We've destroyed Jimmy."

"Is that the leader?" asked Omar.

"Yes," he said, and he introduced himself as Walter. He explained, "Jimmy had promised us a life of wealth and power, but we overheard him saying that once he sold the mooshrooms, he was going to let us go."

The soldier with flaming red hair said, "And that's when we decided to put an end to this."

Walter told the remaining people from the army to go back to their old skins, and one by one they changed from Omar to their real selves.

"We will help you get the mooshrooms back to Mushroom Island," said Walter.

The group walked toward the shore. As they approached Farmer's Bay, they could hear the sounds of mooshrooms mooing.

18
MOOSHROOM STEW

The group worked to build boats and place the remaining mooshrooms aboard. When the final mooshroom was carefully loaded onto the last boat, the gang boarded.

"I'm so glad Mushroom Island will have mooshrooms back," said Dina.

"Now that Jimmy has been destroyed," remarked Allyson, "I hope the hostile mob invasions have stopped."

There was nonstop chatter aboard the ship. Everyone was excited to return to Mushroom Island, and they hoped that it had been restored to its old beauty, which had been peaceful and created a place where people could relax and not live in fear about being terrorized by hostile mobs.

"I wish this ship could move faster," said Allyson. "I can't wait to be back and see what is happening on the island."

Everyone agreed. The trip to the island felt like it lasted forever. They wanted to get to the shore. Omar worried that Jimmy would be on the shore and the battle would start all over again, but he was pleased when they arrived to a dock filled with ships.

Dina was the first person to step off the boat, and she led the final mooshrooms back to their homes. As she walked the animals, the blacksmith rushed from his store and stopped her. "Dina, you're back!"

"Yes, we had to stop the person who was behind these attacks," she replied.

"It looks like you did your job," he remarked. "There hasn't been a hostile mob attack in days, and most of the mooshrooms have returned."

Omar was walking the last mooshroom to its farm when the blacksmith saw him and rushed over to Dina to ask, "What is that thief doing here? Wasn't he the person who was behind all of this?"

Greta sprinted down the grassy path and pulled a diamond sword from her inventory. She pointed it at Omar. "Get off of our island," she hollered.

"No," Dina tried to explain calmly. "This is my friend Omar. He was instrumental in stopping these attacks. He was the one who was the victim. People stole his skin."

"Oh," said the blacksmith. "Now I understand why so many people used to look like him, but they've all changed back to their original skins."

"They're free now," said Omar. "They are no longer doing the bidding of a terrible person."

"I'm sorry that I thought you were the one behind this. I was only trying to defend our island," said Greta.

"Me too," said the blacksmith.

"I understand." Omar smiled and continued to walk the mooshrooms back to the farm.

When Omar reached the farm, Louis the farmer thanked him for returning the mooshrooms. Omar could see Louis was in the process of rebuilding his farmhouse. "It was burned down during the attacks," he explained.

"I'm a builder," said Omar. "I can help you build."

Edison, Billy, Anna, Allyson, Dina, Amira, Peyton, and Erin spotted Omar building the farmhouse with Louis.

"Can we help?" asked Amira.

The group pulled wooden planks and other resources needed to construct the farmhouse. When they were done, Louis thanked them.

"You're welcome," said Omar.

Allyson asked Louis, "Would you like to come over to a party I'm having tonight at my house? We are finally getting to celebrate my friend Amira's birthday."

Amira had forgotten about her birthday party. "Wow, I feel like it's been years since we arrived here to celebrate my birthday. This has been an intense bunch of days."

"Yes, but now we can relax," said Allyson.

Louis accepted the invitation. "I'll bring moosh-room stew."

Edison was pleased. He wanted a bowl of mooshroom

stew, but Peyton, Erin, and Billy put their hands on their stomachs and admitted they still weren't ready to eat a bowl of stew. The competition had ruined their love of the tasty local specialty.

"I'd love one," said Edison.

"Me too," said Anna.

"We will have all types of food at the party tonight," Allyson said, "but we'd love for you to bring the stew."

The gang walked through Mushroom Island toward Amira's house. On the way there, they saw Greta. Allyson invited her to the party. She accepted the invitation.

When they reached Allyson's house, they began to prepare the party. As they set the table with cookies, apples, and cake, Allyson said, "You guys can finally have that vacation you wanted on Mushroom Island."

Edison said, "I think I have to head back tomorrow. I only closed my brewing stand for one week, and I will have customers waiting for potions."

"Well, you'll have to plan another trip," said Allyson.

"I hope the next time we come here, we can relax," added Billy, "I feel like we're always working to solve a mystery. I'm glad this one is over and done."

The gang was still on edge. They waited for the sun to set; once there weren't any hostile mobs spawning in the night, they'd feel like it was officially over.

Dina said, "I know what happened to Mushroom Island was awful, but I have to admit that if it didn't happen, I would have never left the island. I'm not afraid of hostile mobs anymore."

"You're a born fighter. You'd be great to have on a treasure hunt. Would you want to go on one with me?" asked Billy.

"I'd love to go on a treasure hunt," said Dina.

Louis and Greta arrived at the party. The sun had set, and everyone let out a sigh of relief when no hostile mobs spawned.

"We have to celebrate!" said Allyson.

"Happy belated birthday, Amira," said Edison with a smile.

"Thank you." Amira blushed. She wasn't a fan of the attention, but she was glad her friends were able to celebrate with her that night.

Edison pulled out the music disc he had picked up when the charged creeper was destroyed. He played the music as the gang feasted. Through the music, the sounds of mooshrooms were heard in the distance.

The End

WANT MORE OF STEVIE AND HIS FRIENDS?

Read the Unofficial Overworld Adventure series!

Escape from the Overworld
DANICA DAVIDSON

Attack on the Overworld
DANICA DAVIDSON

The Rise of Herobrine
DANICA DAVIDSON

Down into the Nether
DANICA DAVIDSON

The Armies of Herobrine
DANICA DAVIDSON

Battle with the Wither
DANICA DAVIDSON

Available wherever books are sold!